This book belongs to

_____

_____

_____

_____

Age _____

Favourite Fairy Tales

©2006 Alligator Books Limited

Published by Alligator Books Limited
Gadd House, Arcadia Avenue
London N3 2JU

Printed in China

Alice in Wonderland

Alice was beginning to get very tired of sitting by her sister on a grassy bank, and of having nothing to do. The hot day was making her feel very sleepy.

Then, just when she was wondering if she should make a daisy chain, a White Rabbit with pink eyes ran close by her.

There was nothing so very remarkable in that, nor did Alice find it strange when she heard the White Rabbit say to himself, "Oh dear! I shall be late!"

But when the White Rabbit took a watch out of his waistcoat pocket, looked at it and then hurried on, Alice jumped to her feet. For it flashed across her mind that she had never seen a rabbit in a waistcoat holding a watch!

Burning with curiosity Alice ran across the field after him and fortunately was just in time to see him hurry down a large rabbit-hole under the hedge.

In another moment down went Alice after the White Rabbit, never once thinking how she was going to get out again.

The rabbit-hole went straight on like a tunnel for some time, then dipped down suddenly, and Alice found herself falling down a very deep well.

Either the well was very deep, or she fell very slowly, for Alice had plenty of time to look around as she floated downwards.

The sides of the well were filled with cupboards and book-shelves, and here and there she saw maps and pictures hanging on pegs.

Down, down, down she went. Would the fall ever come to an end? Then suddenly, thump, thump, thump! Down she came on a heap of sticks and dry leaves, and the fall was over.

Alice was not hurt a bit and jumped to her feet in a moment. In front of her stretched a long passage, luckily the White Rabbit was still in sight.

Alice sped after him and was just in time to hear him say, "Oh my ears and whiskers, how late it's getting!"

He turned the corner and was gone and Alice found herself in a long low hall.

There were doors all
round the hall. Alice tried
every one, but they were all
locked. Suddenly she saw a
glass table and on the top was
a tiny golden key — but it was
far too small to open any of
the doors.

However, Alice took a second
look and spied a low curtain she
had not noticed before. Behind it
was a small door, which was as
high as her knee. To her delight the
little golden key fit perfectly, and
when Alice knelt down to look straight through the door, she
discovered the most beautiful garden you can ever imagine.

But there seemed no reason at all to wait by the small door,
for Alice couldn't even push her head through the doorway, so she
went back to the glass table.

This time she found a bottle
that had not been there before.
Round the neck of the bottle was
a label marked DRINK ME.

Alice took a sip of the mixture,
it tasted so delicious, she drank
the lot!

"What a curious feeling!" said
Alice as she grew smaller and
smaller. "I must be shutting up
like a telescope."

Now she was just the right size to go through the small doorway into the beautiful garden.

But alas for poor Alice, she had left the little golden key on top of the glass table, and now she could not possibly reach it.

She tried her best to climb up one of the table-legs, but it was far too slippery. Poor Alice sat down and cried.

It was then she noticed a glass box underneath the table. In it was a small cake with the words EAT ME marked on top in currants.

"Well, I'll eat it," said Alice, "and if it makes me grow larger, I can reach the key, and if it makes me grow smaller, I can creep under the door and get into the beautiful garden."

As soon as Alice finished the cake, she grew so large she bumped her head on the ceiling. Poor Alice burst into floods of tears. Now she could only see into the garden with one eye.

She cried so much that a large pool of her tears reached halfway down the hall.

After a while she heard a pattering of feet in the distance. It was the White Rabbit. He got such a fright when he saw the giant Alice, he dropped the fan and gloves he was carrying and scurried away.

Alice picked them up, and as the hall was very hot, she began to fan herself. How strange and muddled she felt sitting all alone in a pool of her own tears.

As she looked down at her hands, Alice was surprised to see that she had put on one of the White Rabbit's little gloves, and it fit perfectly.

"How can I have done that?" she thought. Alice was shrinking rapidly and soon realised it must be the fan, so she dropped it at once.

She was now small enough to go through the door into the beautiful garden at last. But unfortunately the door was locked, and the tiny golden key was back on top of the glass table.

"Things are worse than ever now," sobbed Alice. "I was never as small as this before!"

As she spoke these words, her foot slipped and she was up to her neck in salt water. At first she thought she had fallen into the sea, but she soon realised she had fallen into a pool of her own tears which she had cried when she was huge.

"I wish I hadn't cried so much," said Alice as she swam about.

Then she heard something splashing about in the pool a little way off. At first she thought it was a walrus or a hippopotamus, but when she remembered how small she was, she realised it was only a mouse that had fallen in just like herself.

While Alice was talking to the Mouse and trying to get to know him, several other peculiar creatures joined them in the pool of tears.

Alice thought it was high time to go, so she led the way, and the whole party swam to the shore.

An odd looking Dodo bird held races on the sand, and soon all the creatures were dry.

"Everyone has won, and all must have prizes," said the Dodo bird when the races were finished.

Alice put her hand in her pocket and pulled out a box of sweets, (luckily the salt water had not got into it), she handed them round as prizes, and there was exactly one each.

Later on when Alice began to tell the peculiar creatures about her cat (who caught mice and birds), every one of them hurried away. Alice was left all alone, so she set off to find someone else to talk to.

A great question began to puzzle Alice as she looked at the tall blades of grass around her. "How can I manage to grow big again? I ought to eat or drink something!"

A large mushroom was growing nearby, so she peered over the edge and found herself staring at a blue caterpillar smoking a hookah pipe.

"Who are you?" enquired the Caterpillar sleepily.

"I hardly know!" said Alice. "Being so many different sizes in one day is very confusing!"

"What size do you want to be?" asked the Caterpillar.

"A little larger than I am now," replied Alice (as she was almost the same size as the caterpillar).

"You're a very good height indeed," muttered the Caterpillar as he crawled away. "One side of the mushroom will make you taller, the other side shorter!"

Quickly Alice broke off a piece from either side. When she nibbled the piece in her left hand, she grew taller than the tops of the trees. And when she bit into the piece in her right hand she shrank back to her usual height.

13

As she walked through the woods deciding what to do next, Alice came upon a very small house.

"Anyone who lives here will be frightened out of their wits if they see me this size," thought Alice. So she nibbled the right-hand side of the mushroom until she was small enough to go up to the door.

But when she heard the howling, sneezing and crashing noises that were coming from inside, Alice didn't bother to knock, there was no point!

She pushed open a door that led into a kitchen full of smoke from end to end. A duchess was sitting on a stool nursing a baby, and a cook was leaning over the fire shaking a pepper pot into a pan of soup.

The air was so full of pepper it made Alice sneeze, and the poor baby howled and sneezed without a pause.

A large cat was sitting on the hearth grinning from ear to ear. "Please would you tell me," said Alice, "why your cat grins like that?"

"It's a Cheshire Cat, that's why, Pig!" Alice was quite startled for she thought the Duchess meant her...but it was her baby she was speaking to.

All of a sudden the cook took the pan of soup off the fire and began throwing fire-irons, plates and dishes at the Duchess and the baby.

Alice was really alarmed when the Duchess started to sing a lullaby, at the end of each line she tossed the poor baby up and down until it howled.

"Here! You may nurse it a bit, if you like!" called the Duchess as she flung her baby at Alice. "I must go and get ready to play croquet with the Queen."

Alice caught the wriggling baby and took it outside, and when it began to snort and grunt, Alice looked at its face and found it had turned into a PIG!

So she put the little creature down and it trotted away quietly into the wood.

Alice was suddenly shocked to see the Cheshire Cat sitting grinning on the bough of a tree a little way off.

"Cheshire Puss," she began, "could you tell me, please, which way I ought to go from here?"

"In that direction," said the Cat waving his right paw, "lives a Hatter, and in that direction," waving the other paw, "lives a March Hare. Visit either of them, they're both mad!"

And with that the Cheshire Cat disappeared quite slowly, beginning with his tail and ending with his grin.

Before too long Alice came to the March Hare's house. It was the right place because the chimneys were shaped like ears and the roof was thatched with fur.

A table was set out in the front of the house, and the March Hare and the Hatter were seated at one corner having tea. A dormouse was sitting between them fast asleep, and the other two were using him as a cushion.

"No room! No room!" they cried when they saw Alice coming.

"There's plenty of room!" said Alice indignantly, and she sat down in an armchair at one end of the table.

"What day is it?" the Hatter said to Alice shaking his watch and holding it to his ear.

"The fourth," Alice replied.

"Two days wrong," sighed the Hatter. "I told you butter wouldn't suit the works!" he added, looking angrily at the March Hare.

"It was the best butter," the March Hare meekly replied, then he took the watch and dipped it into his tea.

The March Hare suggested that Alice should tell them a story.

"I'm afraid I don't know one," said Alice.

"Then the Dormouse shall!" they both cried, and pinched him on both sides at once.

The Dormouse opened his eyes and began to tell his tale, but the other two kept moving places and interrupting so often, Alice got up and walked off in disgust.

The Dormouse fell asleep at once, and when Alice looked back, the March Hare and the Hatter had put him in the teapot!

As she went through the wood Alice noticed a door in one of the tree trunks...so she went in. Once more she found herself in the long hall close to the glass table.

"I won't make the same mistake this time," thought Alice and took the golden key and unlocked the small door. Quickly she nibbled a piece of the mushroom that she had kept in her pocket. And when she was small enough, she went through the door straight into the beautiful garden.

A large rose-tree stood near the entrance of the garden. The roses growing on it were white, but three gardeners with bodies like playing cards were busy painting the roses red. Alice was curious to know why.

"Why Miss, this ought to be a red rose, and if the Queen finds out she will have our heads cut off!"

At that moment one of the gardeners called out, "The Queen! The Queen!" and all three began to tremble with fear. The Queen and King of Hearts were approaching. When they reached Alice they stopped and looked at her.

The Queen demanded to know Alice's name. Then she saw the trembling gardeners.

"Off with their heads!" she screamed when she saw the roses covered in red paint.

But the moment the royal party moved off, Alice popped the poor gardeners into a large flowerpot to keep them safe.

19

"Do you play croquet?" shouted the Queen when she noticed Alice again, and when Alice replied that she did, the strangest game began...the balls were live hedgehogs, the mallets live flamingoes, and the soldiers, (who were really cards) had to double themselves up to make the arches.

Alice found it almost impossible to control her flamingo, and the hedgehogs kept unrolling themselves and scampering away.

None of the players waited their turn, they quarrelled all the time and fought over the hedgehogs. In a very short time the Queen was in a furious temper and kept shouting, "Off with his head!" or "Off with her head!" about once a minute.

Alice began to feel very uneasy. "They're very fond of beheading people here. It's amazing there's anyone left alive!"

As she was wondering how she
might escape without being
seen, a curious face appeared in
the air. It was the Chesire Cat.
At least now Alice would have
someone to talk to.

"How do you like the Queen?"
whispered the Cat.

"Not at all," said Alice, but before she
could finish her sentence the King came by.

"I don't like the look of it at all," said the King looking at the
Cat's head with great curiosity, and he called to the Queen to
remove it.

The Queen had only one way of settling this and called for
the executioner. But how can you cut off a head unless it's
attached to a body? And before anyone had time to decide,
the Cat's head faded slowly and was gone.

In the distance a cry was heard, "The trial is beginning!"

"What trial is that?" panted Alice as she
ran to join in with the rest of the crowd.

The King and Queen of Hearts were seated on their thrones when Alice arrived in court.

The Knave of Hearts was standing in front of them in chains, and a large dish of tarts was on a table. In the jury box were twelve creatures all writing busily on slates.

"Herald, read the accusation!" said the King. At this, the White Rabbit blew three blasts on his trumpet and unrolled a scroll.

"The Queen of Hearts she made some tarts,
All on a summer day:
The Knave of Hearts he stole those tarts,
And took them quite away."

The first witness called was the Hatter. As he gave his evidence, Alice realised she was beginning to grow larger.

Can you imagine her surprise when the White Rabbit called Alice as a witness!

Forgetting she was getting bigger by the minute, Alice jumped up and knocked over the jury box.

At this moment the King called out "Silence! All persons more than a mile high must leave the court!"

"Stuff and nonsense!" said Alice loudly.

"Off with her head!" the Queen shouted at the top of her voice.

"Who cares for you?" said Alice (she had grown to full size by now). "You're nothing but a pack of cards!"

At this the whole pack rose up into the air and came flying down on her. Alice gave a little scream and tried to beat them off.

Then Alice heard a faraway voice calling her name, and she found herself lying on the grassy bank, with her head in the lap of her sister, who was gently brushing away some dead leaves that had fluttered down from the trees onto her face.

"Wake up, Alice!" said her sister. "Why, what a long sleep you've had!"

"I've had such a curious dream!" said Alice, and she told her sister all the strange adventures you have just been reading about.

The Adventures of Pinocchio

Once upon a time a woodcutter was chopping a log of wood when suddenly he heard a voice crying, "Stop hitting me you cruel fellow!" The words seemed to come from the log.

The poor man was terrified and ran to find Geppetto the toymaker.

"Oh please take this piece of wood and burn it," begged the woodcutter trembling from head to toe. "I swear it spoke to me!"

Geppetto was delighted as soon as he heard this and had no intention of throwing the log on the fire.

"I'm going to make myself a puppet that looks like a real boy, and this strange log is perfect," Geppetto decided.

So straight away he turned back to his workbench and began to carve the wood.

24

"I shall call my puppet Pinocchio and he will be the son I have always dreamed of."

Poor Geppetto was in for a big surprise! As soon as he had carved Pinocchio's head, the naughty puppet stuck out his tongue.

"You rude boy," scolded Geppetto. "Have you no respect for your father?"

Worse was to come. The second his legs were finished, Pinocchio kicked Geppetto hard then raced out of the door.

"Come back home you wicked boy!" yelled Geppetto shaking his fist angrily as he chased after his puppet.

"What's all this commotion?" hollered a stern looking policeman when Pinocchio leapt into his arms.

"He's trying to run away from me, give him back at once!" shouted Geppetto still very angry.

"Don't you tell me what to do!" snapped the policeman and marched Geppetto off to jail.

Before too long he realized that Geppetto was a kind old man who meant no harm, so he apologized for locking him up and let him go.

Sadly Geppetto made his way back home. "I doubt if I will ever see my Pinocchio again," he sighed.

"I'm so pleased you're back, father," cried a voice the moment Geppetto opened the door. "I'll be a good boy from now on and never run away again!"

At first Geppetto thought it must be a child who lived nearby, but no, it was his own little Pinocchio.

"You can speak just like a real boy," gasped Geppetto and his eyes filled with tears of joy.

That night the old man made Pinocchio some smart new clothes. "Tomorrow you must go to school and learn to read and write as all good boys do."

"I can't go to school without a reading book," gasped Pinocchio the next morning. So although it was bitterly cold, Geppetto rushed outside and sold his only coat to buy a book.

"Thank you, dear father," said Pinocchio as he kissed the old man goodbye. "I promise I will go to school every day and make you proud."

As Pinocchio hurried down the cobbled street he heard music playing. He turned the corner, and there in the middle of the town square, was a travelling theatre.

"Buy a ticket to see *The Great Puppet Show*!" a boy banging on a drum kept shouting.

In an instant Pinocchio forgot all about school and his promise to Geppetto. He sold his reading book for two pennies and bought a ticket to the show.

When Pinocchio saw the puppets singing and dancing he simply had to join in.

At first Enrico, the theatre manager, was extremely angry and tried to throw Pinocchio off the stage, but when the audience started to shower this amazing new puppet with gold coins, he quickly changed his mind!

All that day Pinocchio performed with the other puppets until the theatre closed.

"I've never taken so much money," chuckled Enrico as he handed Pinocchio five gold coins. "Go home to your father, you clever little puppet, and tell him to buy himself a new coat!"

Now Pinocchio did intend to go straight home, but on the way he met a cat pretending to be blind and a fox pretending to be lame. This rascally pair were really two cunning thieves looking for someone to rob.

"Do you want to know how to make your money grow?" asked the cat when he spied Pinocchio's five gold coins.

"We know a place called Miracle Meadow," the fox said. "If you bury your coins there, a tree will grow covered in money."

"Do tell me where it is," pleaded Pinocchio. Then the scheming pair drew closer and whispered in his ear — and the silly puppet believed every word they said.

Off went the cat and the fox at top speed, and as you may have guessed, Pinocchio set off to find the Miracle Meadow and make his fortune.

On the way there a couple of ghostly figures tried to rob him…it was the cat and the fox in disguise of course!

However, Pinocchio was crafty and hid his coins under his tongue. The two thieves were so angry when they failed to find the money, they tied him to a tree and went off empty-handed.

Poor Pinocchio felt so alone and afraid, how he longed to be back home with Geppetto.

Luckily his fortunes were about to change. The Blue Fairy, who helped people in trouble, noticed Pinocchio's plight. She clapped her hands twice and an owl flew down from a tree.

"Untie that unfortunate puppet and bring him to me!" she commanded.

When Pinocchio saw the Blue Fairy, he cheered up at once. Quickly he told her what had happened…but he didn't tell the truth.

As he spoke something extraordinary happened. His nose began to grow! The more lies he told, the longer his nose became.

"Why were you tied to a tree and where is your money?" enquired the Blue Fairy.

"Bandits kidnapped me on my way home, they took my reading book and stole my five coins," lied Pinocchio.
By now his nose was ENORMOUS!

"Tell one more lie and your nose will be longer than a broomstick," warned the Blue Fairy, for she knew none of this had happened and the coins were in his pocket.

"Do what I ask," the Blue Fairy spoke kindly, "then one day I will grant you your dearest wish."

"I want to be a real boy, please!" cried Pinocchio.

"Go home to Geppetto, work hard at school, be truthful and kind and your wish will be granted," promised the Blue Fairy.

Maybe you thought Pinocchio was so grateful to the Blue Fairy that he ran straight home...he did nothing of the kind!

Walking back through Miracle Meadow, he simply couldn't resist burying his coins and waiting for them to grow. Needless to say, the crafty cat and fox were lying in wait ready to steal his money and run away!

When at last Pinocchio returned home, Geppetto was overjoyed and gladly forgave him. For a short while Pinocchio kept the promise he had made. He was truthful and kind, he went to school every single day and learned to read and write.

Unfortunately this was all due to change when he made friends with Tito, the naughtiest, laziest boy in the class.

One day, Tito told Pinocchio about a place called Toyland. "There's no school, and instead of doing dull lessons, everyone lazes around all day," giggled Tito. "A coach leaves at midnight, let's get on it!"

Pinocchio could hardly wait, and late that night as the coach passed through town, both of them climbed aboard.

Strangely the coach looked more like a cage. So many boys were crammed inside, some had to ride on top.

Stranger still, all the donkeys pulling the coach wore boots of white leather tied with laces!

Once in Toyland, Pinocchio and Tito had the time of their lives. No school, no lessons and no teachers…what could be better?

Oddly, none of the boys who arrived on the coach wondered why they had been brought to this place. Before very long they would find out!

As he wandered round Toyland one morning Pinocchio saw, to his horror, that most of the boys had grown long furry ears.

"We're all turning into donkeys!" shrieked Tito.

And when Pinocchio raised his hands to his ears, he screamed with fright too.

"Look! I've grown a tail!" Tito gasped in horror.

"So have I!" Pinocchio began to bray like a donkey.

Sadly that was to be the fate of every naughty boy who had come to live in Toyland…they were turned into donkeys and sold.

Pinocchio was bought by a ringmaster and went to work in the circus. He was taught to jump through hoops, but when he stumbled in the ring and hurt his leg the ringmaster was furious.

"A lame donkey is no good to me. You must go to market and be sold!"

A cruel-looking man who needed a donkey paid a few pennies for Pinocchio. Before the man took him away, Pinocchio made his escape and leapt into the sea.

As he sank beneath the waves he thought of the Blue Fairy and his father Geppetto.

At that very moment something amazing happened. A shoal of coloured fish gently pulled the donkey skin away and Pinocchio was a puppet once more.

It was wonderful!

"Now I am free, I must find my way back home," Pinocchio thought as he swam towards the surface.

All of a sudden a dark shape loomed above him. The shoal of brightly coloured fish fled in terror, for gliding towards Pinocchio was a giant whale.

There was no escape, for as the whale opened his gigantic mouth, Pinocchio was sucked inside and carried down into its stomach.

When the frightened puppet scrambled to his feet he could not believe his eyes.

Inside the whale, rows of golden lights gleamed from the mast of a tiny boat, and a familiar figure was standing inside.

It was his own dear Geppetto alive and well. Pinocchio had never felt so happy.

"Oh how I longed for you to come home. When you never returned," Geppetto explained, "I spent all my days searching for you. There was no trace of you in the town, so I loaded up my boat and put to sea! The whale swallowed me and I've been trapped in here ever since."

"How brave of you, father," said Pinocchio and a big tear rolled down his cheek. "Now we must try to escape."

And escape they did! Showing great courage, Pinocchio managed to control the boat and steer it slowly and carefully out of the whale's stomach.

"We'll soon be free, father!" called Pinocchio boldly, and when the whale rose to the surface and opened his huge mouth, the little boat floated out into the open sea.

Before Geppetto and Pinocchio realised what was happening, a powerful wave washed them onto a sandy beach...and waiting for them was the Blue Fairy.

"Pinocchio," she said gently, "you have shown such love for Geppetto, you truly deserve your dearest wish."

The Blue fairy clapped her hands twice and Pinocchio became a real boy at last.

And so it was, after many adventures and the special magic of the Blue Fairy, Pinocchio was a puppet no more.

Geppetto found the son he had always longed for… and they both lived happily ever after.

The Princess and the Pea

Once upon a time, so the story goes, there lived a certain Prince who longed to be married.

"Remember one important thing," said the Queen rather grandly, "when you find a wife, she must be a *real* princess!" The Prince looked surprised. "What if I fall in love with someone wonderful and she isn't a *real* princess?" he asked in dismay.

"That simply will not do!" snapped the Queen. "She has to be a *real* princess or nothing!"

The Prince glanced at the King who seemed to be shaking his head. "I'm afraid that's how it works when you are a prince," he said quietly.

The Queen, however, did not notice, she was far too busy searching for something in an old oak chest.

"Here it is!" she cried triumphantly. "My list of suitable princesses in every surrounding kingdom!"

The King heaved a long sigh. The Queen, however, did not notice, she was far too busy reading the names on the roll of parchment.

"Visit every single castle on this list and you will be sure to find a *real* princess. Remember nothing less will do!" And these were the Queen's last words on the subject.

So without further delay, the Prince set off on his search for a bride.

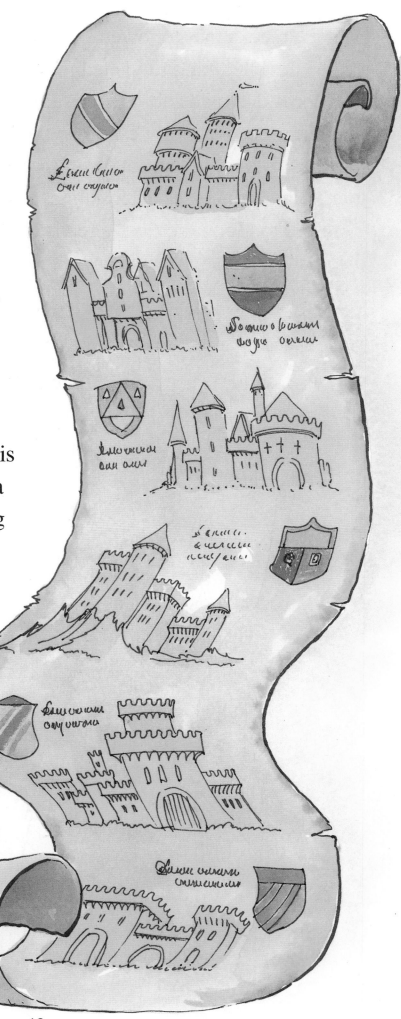

In the weeks that followed the Prince travelled far and visited many kingdoms. He made absolutely sure that he stopped at every castle on the Queen's list and he introduced himself to as many princesses as possible.

Before too long the Prince realised that his task was far from easy.

Some of the princesses seemed rather old, while others seemed far too young, and some of the castles were in ruins. This made the Prince wonder if the Queen's list was out of date.

There were some princesses, with absolutely no manners at all, who giggled and tittered the moment they saw him. It was very embarrassing.

He called on one princess who was so bad-tempered, she refused to open the castle door. Worse still, she pulled faces and yelled at him from the balcony!

Sadly the Prince lost all hope of ever finding a *real* princess he could marry. So feeling very tired and disappointed, he threw away the Queen's list and headed for home….now it so happened that right at the very bottom of the Queen's list was a magnificent castle which the Prince failed to see.

Could it be that the *real* princess he was seeking lived inside?

Now he may never know!

The Prince looked so sad when he returned to the castle alone, so the King tried his best to cheer him up.

"One day soon you will meet a princess that you really love, of that I am certain!" he assured him.

The Queen, on the other hand, remained quite firm.

"Tomorrow you must set off once more, and this time you have to try harder," she said crossly. "You can not expect a *real* princess to come knocking on the door!"

Later that night there was a terrible storm. Thunder shook the castle and lightning seemed to split the skies.

The Prince felt pleased to be back home safe and warm beside a blazing fire.

Then, above the sound of rain pouring and wind howling down the chimney, a knock was heard.

"Who could possibly be visiting us on such a wild night?" asked the Queen.

Straight away the King rose from his chair. "No need to summon the servants," he said, "I will go myself and see who is at the door."

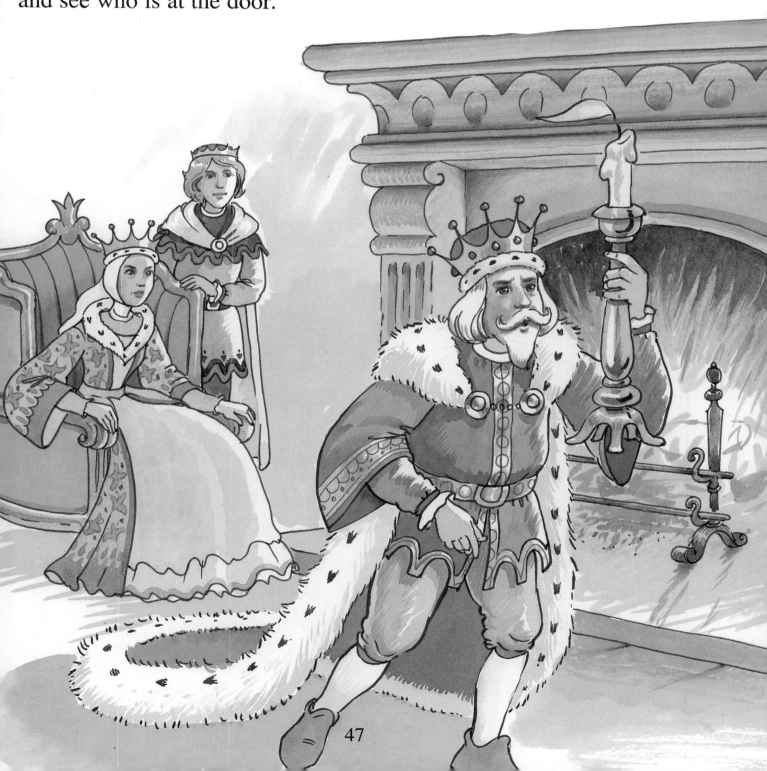

To his amazement, the King found a beautiful young girl in the doorway. The poor thing was shivering with cold, her clothes were soaked and her shoes splattered with mud.

"Come inside at once, my dear!" The King had to shout loudly to be heard above the noise of the gale.

Quickly he slammed the door, and then led the stranger into the castle to warm herself by the fire.

And in that moment the Prince fell deeply in love with her. At long last he had met the girl he wanted to marry.

"What brought you to the castle on a night like this?" enquired the King.

"Your Majesty," she replied dripping from head to toe, "My name is Princess Adelina. As I was riding back home through your kingdom, darkness fell and I was caught in the storm."

"Do go on, my dear," said the Queen, for she had heard the word *princess* and was eager to find out more.

"All in good time," said the King. "First our guest must be given dry clothes or she could catch a cold, and I'm sure a bowl of hot soup would make her feel better!"

"She doesn't look like a *real* princess to me," muttered the Queen under her breath, "but I know how to tell if she is genuine or not!"

So the Queen, determined as ever, rushed off to wake her servants who were already in bed at such a late hour.

In the meantime, a cosy fur-trimmed gown was found for the Princess to wear, and a pair of dainty slippers that fitted perfectly. Her long chestnut hair was dry now, and as the Prince gazed at this beautiful girl in the firelight, he was enchanted.

When she had finished supper, Princess Adelina told how her horse was startled by the thunder and had galloped off in the wrong direction.

"When I saw the lights shining from your castle windows, I rode up to the gates to find shelter," the Princess explained. "One of your grooms saw me and took my horse into the royal stables for the night."

And as the three sat comfortably by the fire, Princess Adelina listened spellbound to the King's stories about his kingdom, the Prince fell more and more in love with her every minute.

Meanwhile, the Queen ordered her sleepy servants to make up a very special bed. "Bring me twenty of the firmest mattresses you can find!" she commanded.

The servants were bewildered at her strange request, but of course they obeyed.

Preparing the bed took ages, for the heavy mattresses had to be brought from every corner of the huge castle. Some of them were carried, some of them were pulled, while others were pushed and shoved.

"Place one on top of another," the Queen told her servants. Then when no one was looking, she popped a tiny dried pea under the first mattress.

"Now we shall see if Princess Adelina is a *real* princess or not!"

Before too long the pile of mattresses had grown so high, special steps were brought to reach up to the top.

"How truly splendid!" cried Princess Adelina when she saw her bed. "You should not have gone to all this effort for me!"

"No trouble at all," said the Queen as she watched the Princess climb up the steps. "Goodnight and sweet dreams, my dear."

"This bed looks so comfortable," Princess Adelina called down from the top of the twentieth mattress, "I shall fall asleep the moment my head touches the pillow!"

"We shall see," whispered the Queen as she closed the door.

During the night the terrible storm passed. The wind died down, the rain stopped, the thunder rolled away and all was peace and quiet.

Everyone in the castle was fast asleep except for Princess Adelina.

Her bed was so uncomfortable she tossed and turned all night long, and by morning she hadn't had a wink of sleep.

The poor girl was so tired, she could scarcely get out of bed and climb down the steps for breakfast.

"Did you sleep well, my dear?" the Queen asked eagerly the moment Princess Adelina came into the room.

"I'm afraid I did not," replied the Princess trying her best not to yawn.

The Queen held her breath.

"There was a small hard lump under my mattress," the Princess explained as she rubbed her sore back. "Perhaps it was a marble, or a bead, or a button that kept me awake all night."

"It was a pea!" cried the Queen with delight.

"A pea?" the King frowned.

"A pea?" the Prince gasped.

"A pea?" Princess Adelina looked puzzled.

"Yes, a tiny dried pea!" laughed the Queen. "Only a *real* princess would have a skin so tender that she could feel a tiny pea through twenty mattresses.

"I knew she was a *real* princess the second I met her!" cried the King joyfully.

"It never mattered to me," sighed the Prince as he gazed into Princess Adelina's eyes.

"I am so sorry I ever doubted you," said the Queen, and she threw her arms round the Princess and gave her a kiss.

"You were not to blame at all," Princess Adelina spoke to the Queen in the kindest way. "For who would expect a *real* princess to come knocking at the door on such a terrible night?"

Happily everything turned out well. The Prince asked the Princess if she would consent to be his bride, and she willingly agreed.

For as she told the King and Queen that morning, she had already fallen hopelessly in love with their son the moment she came in from the storm.

Later on, the Prince brought Princess Adelina her horse from the royal stable, and side by side they rode away to her parents' kingdom.

"I must have visited every castle in my search for a bride! How could I have missed this one?" the Prince thought to himself as they came in sight of Princess Adelina's home.

Now as you may recall, this magnificent castle was right at the bottom of the Queen's list...*and the Prince had thrown it away!*

But thanks to a terrible storm and a tiny dried pea, this story has a perfect ending. The Prince and Princess married amid great rejoicing, and they lived happily ever after.

Princess Adelina made sure that the tiny dried pea was placed inside a special glass case, and there it remained for all to see.

And to this day, the story of the Princess and the Pea is often told in front of warm fires...especially on dark and stormy nights.

The Adventures of Sinbad

Many years ago in an ancient eastern city there lived a young man whose name was Sinbad. His father, who was very rich, died and left his son a great deal of money. But in a short while Sinbad had foolishly wasted most of his father's wealth.

With what little money he had left, Sinbad decided to buy goods to trade in other lands. So he boarded a ship with several other merchants and put to sea.

"Our fortunes will be made on this voyage!" Sinbad called cheerfully to the men as the ship sailed out of the harbour.

Time went by and Sinbad's ship journeyed far across the ocean.

Wherever it stopped, at ports or islands, people were eager to buy the merchant's goods in return for gold and silver, and Sinbad became a rich man once more.

One day, as the ship was passing a small island, the captain suggested that everyone might like to go ashore. Sinbad and the others had only been there for a short while when the whole island started to shudder and shake.

Suddenly, out of the water, rose the gigantic head of a sea monster! Fortunately the terrified men were thrown off its back before the monster dived beneath the waves.

The moment the captain thought everybody had returned safely to the ship he set sail, but in the confusion Sinbad was left behind clinging to a piece of wood.

And before that day was out, the swift current had taken him to the shores of another island.

Soon enough, Sinbad was discovered and taken before the King who ruled the island. The King was so impressed that Sinbad had managed to stay alive, he gave him a chest full of gold and a fast ship to carry him home.

Although Sinbad returned to his city a very rich man, he soon grew bored and longed for further adventures. Then one day a group of merchants asked Sinbad to join them on their next voyage.

All went well until they landed on a faraway desert island, where, by some strange chance, Sinbad was left behind once more. And when he gazed out to sea from the top of a palm tree, the ship was almost out of sight.

It was then he noticed a giant white ball near the beach, so he climbed down to investigate. Suddenly out of the sky a gigantic bird flew towards him. (He had often heard sailors tell of a fearsome bird called a Roc.)

As soon as the Roc sat down on its huge egg, Sinbad tied himself to the bird's leg with his turban, and when the Roc took off, Sinbad was carried away from the desert island.

The Roc flew high over the sea, and on reaching the mountains, it swooped down into a deep valley.

When the giant bird landed, Sinbad just managed to untie the knot of his turban before the Roc seized a serpent in its beak and flew away.

Sinbad looked about him and saw that the ground was covered in enormous diamonds, but coiled between the gems lay massive serpents dozing in the sun.

As he stood holding his sword in case the serpents awoke, something fell from the cliffs high above. When Sinbad glimpsed men standing on top of the cliffs, he quickly worked out what was happening.

They were hurling large pieces of meat onto the diamonds below, for they knew that the mountain eagles would fly down. The gems would stick to the meat, and then be carried back to the eagles' nests, where the men could collect them.

Now Sinbad knew of a way to escape! He picked up the biggest diamond and stuck it onto a piece of meat, and when the next eagle swooped down, he grabbed its legs and was carried out of the valley to safety.

And so it was, when Sinbad returned home, he was able to sell the magnificent diamond he had brought from the Valley of the Serpents and give the money to the poor in his city.

Sinbad had only been back for a while when he began to find life rather dull, so he chartered a ship and set sail once more.

After travelling for many days, the ship ran into a terrible storm. Very soon strong winds and towering waves drove it close to an island.

Before Sinbad and the other sailors could swim to the shore, hordes of savage creatures clambered up the sides of the ship and swarmed all over the deck.

Sinbad and the rest of the men were overpowered and dragged off to a castle on the island.

They were taken before a hideous giant with one bulging eye that stared out of the middle of his forehead.

"Perhaps they will hold us for ransom or make us work as slaves," whispered Sinbad.

That night they were locked up in prison, and next morning were sent to work in the giant's forest. Seeing so many logs lying on the ground gave Sinbad an idea!

In the days that followed, whenever the guards turned their backs, the sailors built rafts that they managed to hide.

Late one night, when the guards had fallen asleep, Sinbad and his friends made their escape from the castle. They hurried down to the shore where the rafts were hidden, jumped aboard and rowed quickly away from that awful island.

Most of the rafts were large and could carry several men. One raft was smaller than the rest, but it was big enough for Sinbad.

As the men pulled on their oars and sped swiftly into the darkness, Sinbad's raft was caught in a whirlpool!

The raft spun round and round then vanished, and poor Sinbad was tossed into the raging sea. Luckily by morning he had been washed up on a beach.

As he came to his senses Sinbad heard a hissing sound. Slithering across the beach was a huge serpent!

In fear for his life, Sinbad climbed to the top of the nearest tree with the serpent close behind.

By great good fortune, some sailors on a passing ship heard Sinbad's desperate cries. They sent a boat to pick him up and frightened off the serpent with a hail of arrows.

With Sinbad safely aboard, his rescuers listened in awe to his incredible story. Then, without any warning, a powerful wave dashed the ship against a jagged rock. Sinbad and the crew had scarcely time to jump off before the ship sank near an island.

The water was shallow, and when the men waded ashore, they discovered hundreds of chests overflowing with treasure – so many ships had been wrecked in that place and their valuable cargo washed up on the beach.

With all that treasure spread before them, the men could go home rich beyond their wildest dreams.

But unfortunately they had been shipwrecked at the foot of a high mountain with sides too steep to climb!

Sinbad was puzzled. A vast river of dark water flowed *from* the sea and disappeared through a cavern into the mountain.

"Could this be a means to escape?" wondered Sinbad.

When he explained to the men
what he planned to do, without a
moment's hesitation, they gathered
up the ship's timber that littered
the shore and built a strong raft,
and on top they loaded a cargo of
gold and precious stones.

"When I reach safety, I promise
to send a ship for you and the rest
of the treasure!" called Sinbad as
he leapt aboard.

Swiftly the river took him
through the mouth of the
cavern and deep into
the mountain.

The water swept the raft along. Very soon Sinbad found himself in total darkness and after many hours he fell into a deep sleep.

When he awoke it was daylight. A group of people on the bank were surprised to see a stranger floating by. They tied his raft to a tree, and brought a fine horse for Sinbad to ride to the city of Serendib to meet the King.

The first thing the King did when he had listened to Sinbad's story was to send a ship to rescue the sailors still left behind.

During the days that followed, Sinbad and the King became great friends. And when Sinbad left for his own city, the King entrusted him with a letter of friendship and costly gifts for his ruler, the Caliph, so great was his faith in Sinbad.

72

After a long journey Sinbad reached home. Straight away he delivered the letter and gifts to the Caliph, who was delighted.

"You must go back to the King of Serendib with gifts from me in return for his friendship."

So Sinbad was forced to set sail once more, as the Caliph could not be disobeyed. When he arrived in Serendib, the King was overjoyed to see Sinbad again, and was greatly honoured by the Caliph's gifts.

But alas, on the way home, Sinbad's ship was attacked by pirates!

They took the ship and all the treasure that had been loaded on board from the King of Serendib.

The pirates captured Sinbad and the crew and chained them up in the hold. Worse still, they were sold as slaves in the next port.

Sinbad was bought by a wealthy merchant and taken to join the rest of his many servants. Although he was now a slave, his life was not hard.

The merchant had a beautiful daughter named Yasmin, and as the time passed Sinbad fell in love with her.

One early morning the merchant sent for Sinbad. "Slave! I have a special task for you. In the forest lives the biggest of all elephants. Tonight, when the moon shines full, he will come to drink at the pool nearby. Take this bow and arrow and shoot him, or I will have you killed!"

Sinbad was horrified for he knew the merchant wanted the elephant's valuable ivory tusks to sell. What was he to do?

That night Sinbad set off towards the forest as the merchant had ordered.

On reaching the pool, Sinbad hid behind a large rock and waited. As he watched he saw the great elephant striding out of the forest. Its long curved tusks gleamed in the moonlight as it waded into the water.

Sinbad stepped forward cautiously, then he saw to his astonishment, the merchant's beautiful daughter sitting on the elephant. At first when Yasmin noticed Sinbad she was very upset.

"My father is a cruel man. That is why I come here at night to protect this gentle creature," she cried. "Shoot me instead! For I would rather die myself than let this beautiful elephant die!"

"Tonight I came to the pool to *save* the elephant," explained Sinbad. "I know your father is waiting for me to bring back its ivory tusks, but I planned to ride away on the elephant to freedom."

Yasmin had never felt happier in her life when she heard what Sinbad said, for now her beloved elephant would be saved from the cruellest of fates.

"I have no wish to return to my father," sighed Yasmin, "but where shall I go?"

"Come and live in my city," said Sinbad. Yasmin gladly agreed (for secretly she had fallen in love with him the moment he was brought to the house as a slave).

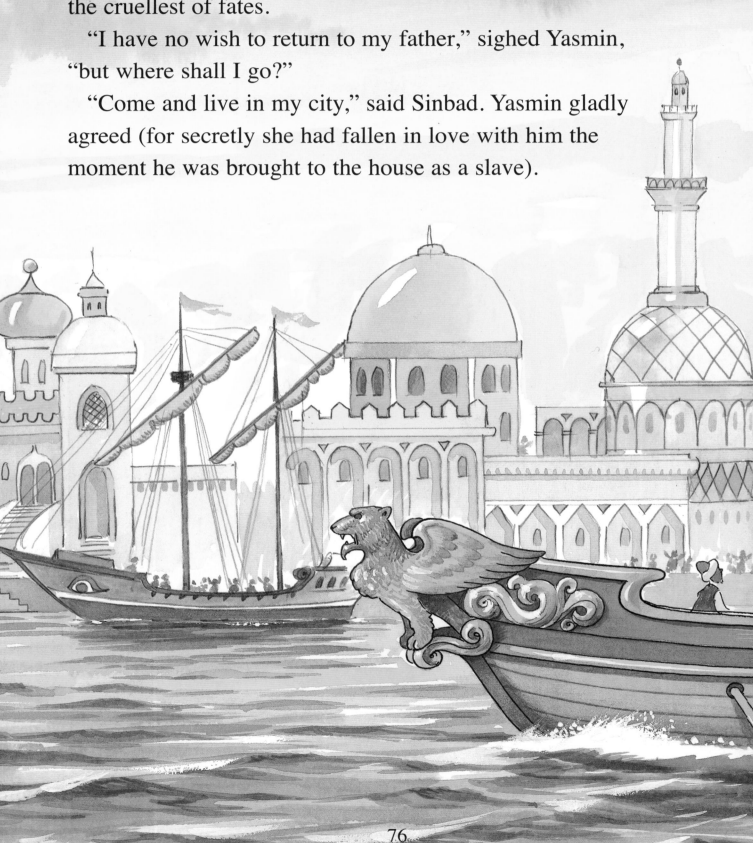

The two journeyed through many different lands, they travelled across hot deserts, wide plains and high mountains, but Yasmin and Sinbad were safe every step of the way on the back of their elephant.

When they came in sight of Sinbad's city, the Caliph's own barge was waiting to carry them across the water.

Great were the celebrations when people saw the golden barge arrive, for Sinbad had come home at last.

When tales of his incredible adventures were told, Sinbad became famous throughout the land.

He never put to sea again and gave most of the riches he had made from his voyages to the poor…and Yasmin and Sinbad lived happily ever after.

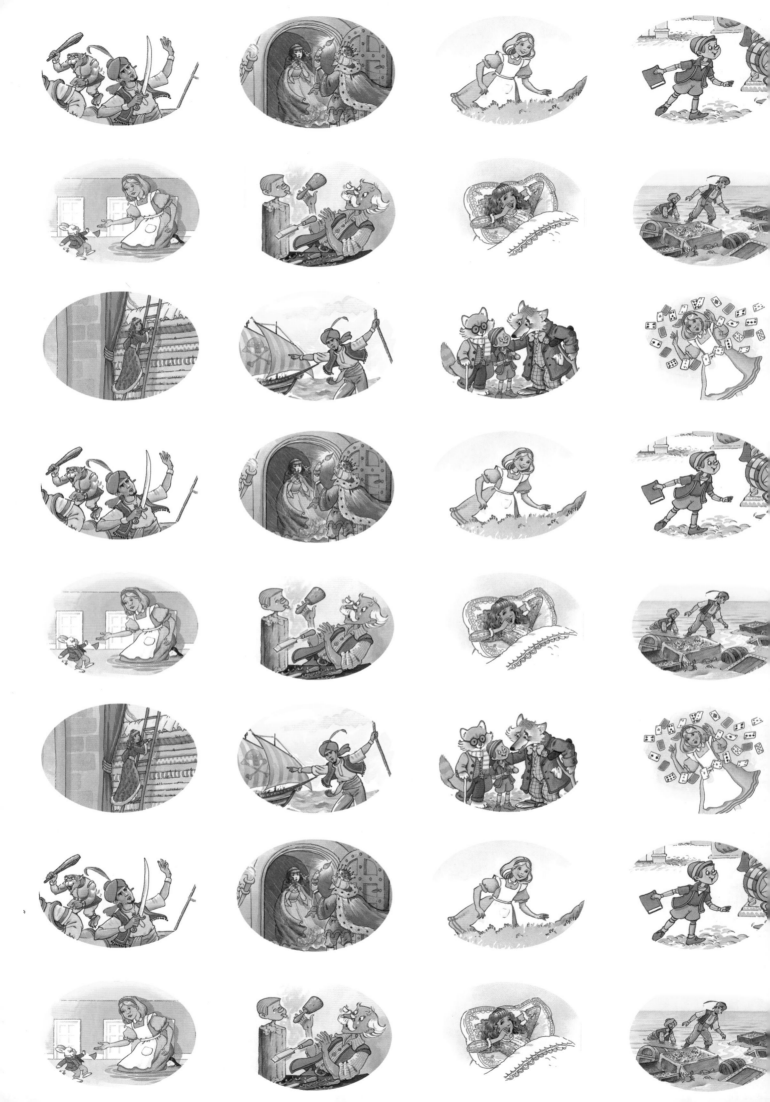